hor

GH00786584

Dangero

Welsh Arts Council

Penny Windsor was brought up in the West Country but has lived in Swansea for twenty years and regards it as her home. She has mainly worked as a teacher and youth worker but now works as the South Wales Advisory Officer for the National Association of Citizens Advice Bureaux.

She has been involved in the Women's Movement for many years, particularly working with young women and teaching women and literature courses. Besides writing, other 'obsessions' are swimming and long distance walking.

She is now forty, mother of a teenage daughter. She says 'I have been writing poetry since I was four years old; since I could write'.

Dangerous Women

Penny Windsor

honno

Published by Honno, 'Ailsa Craig', Heol y Cawl, Dinas
Powys, South Glamorgan, CF6 4AH.

First impression 1987

© Penny Windsor, 1987

British Library Cataloguing in Publication Data

Windsor, Penny
    Dangerous Women.
    I. Title
    821'.914   PR6073.I49

    ISBN 1-870206-02-9

All rights reserved.

Published with the financial support of the Welsh Arts
Council.

The Publishers would like to acknowledge the assistance and
guidance of the Design Department of the Welsh Books
Council which is supported by the Welsh Arts Council.

Cover Design: Rhiain Davies

Printed in Wales by Qualitex Printing Ltd., Cardiff

Contents

Some of the poems in this collection have appeared in the following magazines, publications and anthologies: *Outwrite, Spare Rib, Poetry Wales, No Holds Barred, Green Horse*. Also, some of the poems have been read on Radio Wales, Swansea Sound, HTV and Thames Television.

Women are in danger
            walking the streets
            in public houses
            travelling alone
            at nights in the city
We have our own ways of fighting back
            hiding behind smiles
            secret everyday lives
            fantasies
            scribbled messages on serviettes
We are making a journey
the Mothers and daughters
the Women-in-the Street
"Like a grand sailing ship
with the wind behind it"
We are "making for the open".

Women are dangerous
            We turn knitting into a subversive activity
            write notes to our Daughters that nobody else
                understands
            advise each other on contraception and
                pregnancy and child-care
            compare experiences about jobs and
                interviews
            "paint on the inside covers of our children's
                books"
            realize beauty is nothing but an elusive dream
            celebrate the passing of the years

We are dangerous
because we are all Mothers and Daughters
We are dangerous
because now We have no need "to ask anything at all"
We are dangerous
because We have found many different ways
to celebrate
being a Woman.

part one

the street poems

Things Men Say

men in the street say funny things
here are some of their sayings
"get 'em off"
"hello big tits"
"fancy a fuck darling"
"smile"
"get it up there"
"your place or mine"
this is a brief selection

now, I don't want to be difficult
unappreciative
I know these are all sayings
that mean I'm desirable
wanted by men
in a man's world
this is obviously a good thing

and it's not that I want
intellectual conversation
or the New Man's heavy sensitivity
or even gems of common wisdom from the building site —
but I do feel
and I don't want to offend anyone
the standard's a bit low

I'm sorry for all this
because I know men try
they really do

and it's very confusing to know what women want
but I think — and I do apologise
that these sayings
don't . . . amuse or excite me
or even make me feel . . . attractive
and if I'm completely honest
and don't misunderstand me
I'm not a feminist
if I'm completely honest
these sayings irritate
in fact
they make me Angry
yes, ANGRY
I wish those men would stuff their little sayings . . .
in their lunch box

sorry about that

Public House

The stranger stares
is she free?
is she trouble?
is she mine?

no, I say, I'm here to read my poetry
I play piano here
I write reviews for local magazines
Strictly Business
the stranger understands

but should I say I'm here for fun
for pleasure
to relax and have a good time
the stranger leers

she can't enjoy herself
she must be desperate
she must have no choice
yes, that's it
must save her from herself
end her desperation
pleasure her
see she has a good time

when I leave
the stranger creeps into the street
after all, I had no business there.

Smile

"Smile" they said
the men on building sites
the boys at school
strangers on the street
"Give us Give us
Give us a smile"

I learned to smile
and was their love
their duck, their chick
their oh so happy little flower

I learned it like an animal
who needs its owner's food and warmth
I learned it as a girl
searching out the ways to please, succeed
and when I grew
I learned to carry it around
a handy little, deadly little, smile

Now when they jeer at me
for wearing out-of-fashion clothes
and when they leer at bits of me
as though my breasts and legs
did not belong to me
I bare my teeth and spread my lips
give them a smile

The Curfew

It's curfew time, girls.
The streets are getting dark.
it's stop-tap,
the clubs are closing down.
Put on your shrouds
and hurry
hurry home.

It's curfew time, girls.
Those particularly at risk
are those with large breasts
long hair
tight trousers
full-length dresses
T-shirts
make-up
fresh complexions
stockings, tights, popsocks
jewellery
or those wearing badges expressing or publicising opinions
    of any kind.

It's curfew time, girls.
The streets are full
of men
frustrated men who need girls like you
desperately
violent men who hate girls like you
profoundly
drunken men who know they own girls like you
eternally.

It's curfew time, girls.
Next time you want
to visit a friend
eat out
drink in a pub
attend an evening class
take the dog to the park
jog
go to a film

remember

you are putting *yourself* at risk
any assault
sexual or otherwise
is *your* fault
and any attempt
to reclaim the night
for everybody's use
will lead to violent opposition
from all men
who drink, grope, rape
beat up women
expose themselves
or pass obscene remarks.
An impressive opposition girls
powerful
important.

It's curfew time, girls.
Stake your claim
in the home
don't venture out
stay
behind locked doors.

A Simple Woman's Guide to Politics

If we could get them all together —
tyrant teachers and righteous preachers
pompous MPs, Heads of State, money men
tin god bosses in office blocks
puffed up clerks
rule makers
war mongers
women haters —
invited
to a gathering of the world's important people
for free and frank discussion
of the future . . .
we could lock the door
set the themes (peace, equality and sisterhood)
and, not waiting for the ponderous reports
about how things could change a hundred years from now
— let the bastards rot
snatch their loot
plagiarise their power
and run free and laughing
to the lovely, bitter end.

Places I've Been Banned From (in Swansea)

I've been banned from the Rank for joining in a fight
and living on Townhill —
and banned from the Cricketers
for shouting at the manager
for shouting at a friend —
and I've been banned from the Townsman
for kicking men who said "smile, it hasn't happened yet"
and warned away from County Hall
for saying it should be bombed
in a letter to a man in education

I've been banned from couples' "dos"
because I am divorced
and banned from married homes
because I live in sin
and I'm not really welcome
in shops, in pubs, in conferences
because I have a child
or cafes
because I have a dog
or Berni Inns
because I'm vegetarian
and I'm treated as a trifle suspect
by the Left
because I'm feminist
by CND
because I go to Greenham
by serious and deadly workers-in-the-field
for writing poetry

and recently
well, recently
I've been banned from The Coach House
for *reading out* my poetry

So, if I could only give up
the poetry, the politics, the feminist beliefs
the dog, the man, the child
the running wild
I'd be — Home and Dry —
which is why
I don't

on a paper serviette

the barmaid bit her nails
a glass of brandy tipped

the boss-man scowled
hung his gut upon the bar
and growled

the barmaid sighed
"the city where you live, how near?
how much is it to fly?
have I enough, or is it very dear?
draw a map" she cried

the boss-man scowled
hung his gut upon the bar
and howled

but the barmaid
safe now with dreams and schemes
could afford to let
the brandy drip and stay
as she planned
the details of her get-away . . .
on a paper serviette

over to you W. H.

"what is this life if full of care
we have no time to stand and stare?"
W.H. Davies —

a foolish sentiment
written by a male poet

have you tried it lately
standing and staring?

W.H. just didn't comprehend
women aren't allowed

they are picked up, put away or put down

"what is this life men do not care
we have no right to stand and stare?"

over to you W.H.

Some Observations about Women Travelling Alone

women can eat at a cafe or restaurant
women can't picnic in a public square
can — drink coffee in a cafe but not beer in a bar

women can sit and read, or write a novel
but women can't just sit

women can walk quickly and purposefully in one particular
    direction
but they can't go past the same place twice within a short time
    for no apparent reason
or stand still for no apparent reason
women can stand still if they look at a historic building or in a
    shop window

women can go out after dark to visit relatives or do late night
    shopping
they cannot walk round generally after dark

they can travel with a particular and worthy and feminine
    reason in mind
such as collecting butterflies
but they cannot travel to wander or merely to sightsee

women can wear loose clothes in dark or pastel shades
but not tightfitting and revealing clothes in any colour
or loose clothes in bright colours

women can smile and look directly at children and dogs
women cannot smile or look directly at men

women by themselves can mention their husbands,
    boyfriends, children with fondness and regret
they cannot say they are alone by choice
oh no, they can never say they are alone by choice

Give Me Love in Winter

Give me love in winter
when the bed is cold
and the frost is biting at my lips
With love I could look kindly
on a hundred barren trees
and pointless streets
and all those faded days
that shudder to a pinched and sombre climax
somewhere in December.

Give me love in winter
and I would treat
the season's vagaries
with a fine indifference,
calling to you
on the fierce white air
that we alone
should see these dead months through
and watch the sun rise
on a milk and honey land.

Give me love in winter
then and only then.
For I shall meet you
on a pavement
in the spring
and, self-sufficient,
pass you with a nod.
No grief or pleading
stories told of what we did.
I will discard you
like an old, worn hat,
saying, "fool, it was a passing love".
The thought of winter
makes dependents of us all.

Time Off

I'm putting off going home
because I'll think about the cleaning
I'm putting off going home
because the kids are screaming
I'm putting off going home
because it's stark reality
and I'm dreaming and scheming
about adventures and romances —
a mutual seduction
with a man that makes good pizzas
an exotic unplanned journey
on Mumbles railway
with the moon over Swansea Bay

I'm putting off going home
because inside I'm screaming
I want more than cleaning dust up
and weekly treats that must
be quick and cheap
and I'm not really fussed
if I never see the place again

I know I'm only dreaming
and that bliss is over-rated
and romance is slightly dated
but I say — sod it to the cleaning
I want to go on dreaming
I'm putting off going home today.

Heroines

We are the terraced women
piled row upon row on the sagging, slipping hillsides of our
    lives
We tug reluctant children up slanting streets
the push chair wheels wedging in the ruts
breathless and bad tempered we shift the Tesco carrier bags
    from hand to hand
and stop to watch the town

the hill tops creep away like children playing games

our other children shriek against the schoolyard rails
"there's Mandy's mum, John's mum, Dave's mum, Kate's
    mum, Ceri's mother, Tracey's mummy"
we wave with hands scarred by groceries and too much
    washing up
catching echoes as we pass of old wild games

after lunch, more bread and butter, tea
we dress in blue and white and pink and white checked
    overalls
and do the house and scrub the porch and sweep
    the street
and clean all the little terraces
up and down and up and down and up and down the hill

later, before the end-of-school bell rings
all the babies are asleep
Mandy's mum joins Ceri's mum across the street
running to avoid the rain
and Dave's mum and John's mum — the others too — stop
    for tea
and briefly we are wild women
girls with secrets, travellers, engineers, courtesans, and stars
    of fiction, films
plotting our escape like jail birds
terraced, tescoed prisoners rising from the household dust
like heroines.

The Journey

I

The Greyhound bus at the farthest bay
was the through bus to Cheyenne, Wyoming.
I staggered through the swing doors of the waiting room
with my rucksack and the sleeping child,
and down the long, high entrance hall.
It was past midnight and the shops and ticket office
were closed. I saw drunks and drug addicts
and police with hands on their guns.
A woman shouted into a dead phone.

(Some time ago, waiting, I wrote you a letter
but, cursing me for leaving you alone, you probably
   wouldn't reply)
I checked my ticket, stowed my luggage, lay the sleeping
   child across my knees
listened to a woman high on drugs, argue with the driver.

We roared from the station, glided from the city
took to the freeway across the northern plains.
The argument went on. I took a travel sickness pill
and tried to feel my numbed legs.

I thought "you would like this: you would make a speech or
   write a poem"
In the night I remembered your strong arms and hard body
and looked for a long time at your features on the face of the
   child.

But near Cheyenne it was daylight and the sun
burned the lonely green towns in the desert.
The child spoke.
I remembered then your face twisted with rage
and saw myself sitting still with fear
hundreds of miles away.

II

I stayed for several weeks in the mountains above Denver.
There was a friend here from my university days.
The cabin was high like a church and full of sun.

I sat in pools of light writing your long letters
on my friend's old typewriter, and hurried across the stream
to put them in the mailing box — Salina Star Route 80602.

The child made crumbling castles in the dry soil,
sang nursery-rhyme songs and floated pine needles in the
    water.

Only during the hot nights did I grow restless
my body twisting away from your image.

III

When the brief summer ended I went south
to New Mexico where the freeways seemed wet with heat.
I walked in the desert among the shrubs and rats.
The child's face grew pink and she resisted my hot embrace.

I remembered how we tried to touch
the long, hot months before I left
but irritated by the heat and by our wretched pasts
I had gone to sleep with the child in the room next door
and gradually we had neither spoken nor touched
the heat between us like a wall.

I found Sante Fe at the far edge of the desert
a green town among blue mountains.
The people spoke Spanish and some sold bright Indian
    trinkets
in the elegant square. I drank Tequila
and watched the child chalking numbers on the street
and drunk, thought of you drunk, and your ugly eyes
as you called me "bitch" and tried to throw me out.

IV

In New York I shrank among the buildings
hiding in the top storey of a hostel on 42nd street.
But I couldn't shut out the wailing sirens nor the cries
of the mad woman next door who saw a hundred bodies
crushed each night in a subway disaster.
I let the child eat ice-cream every day
in the multi-flavoured ice-cream parlours, took her to the
    Children's Zoo in Central Park
and pampered her with books and toys.

Knowing the journey must end — I had to work, the child go
    to school —
I went to Kennedy Airport one night and quietly
left America.

V

We wept when we met and I was afraid again —
there had been no letters from you.

you had found us a rented flat near the sea front
and we made love there throughout the night.

When the child woke we walked on the wide beach
in the rain.

But I could not forgive the fear you made me feel
and you could not forget those lonely summer months
when I was gone, and before then the months I
    slept alone
and, in the rain, we began to argue and the child looked up
and started to cry.

Celebration One:
Making for the Open

swimming in the fast lane
the water caresses my skin
like silk
I am not just afloat
not just drifting
as one might on a sunny day
in the sea
I am like a grand sailing ship
with the wind behind it
making for the open
sailing to the sky

swimming in the fast lane
the water slips from my skin
as easily as rain
I stroke it away and around
and back to me
testing and teasing and tickling
The water is mine
colluding in my getaway
tempting
with the sweetness of my strength
the beguiling rhythm of my limbs
seductive soft-green strokes

swimming in the fast lane
I know I will not be back
I am making for the open
faraway places where no one has ever been

one day soon
I will swim to the sky

part two

the mother-daughter poems

dear mam

dear mam
i'm out
love sian
dear mam
can i stay the night with al?
see you soon
sian
mam
disco at the rank
staying at kate's
is this o.k.?
p.s.
can i have my pocket money?

sian
please take, dog out
and do washing up
love mam
dear sian
working late seeing jen back nine
see you mam
sian
paid today
prepare for Great Food Expedition
mam

mam
broke bottle of wine
sorry
smells lovely
gareth called

i said no
more spot cream please
and gel
dogs weren't allowed

mam
i've borrowed your jumper
the one with sleeves
gareth called again
he's nice but small
i fancy steve
he's going with kate
back at ten
love sian

sian
where's my jumper?
has gareth grown?
who's steve?
how's school?
washing up
back soon
love mam

dear mam
dear sian
see you soon
love sian
love mam

Have Faith in your Daughter

One day in June last summer
I found I was the Rose Queen's mother
Of course I had said, "but looks don't count
It's kindness, character", — but she'd found out
Ways of dealing with feminist mums.

All freckles, Celtic charm and cheek
She won, leaving me on the day, the freak
Of the show, while she, in satin gown and crown
Enjoyed the fuss as prettiest girl in town,
And it was, in its way, a classic occasion.

Teacakes and teacups, side stalls and sun
A stern-looking vicar disapproving of fun
A local JP with friends in high places and fingers in pies
Giving out prizes, telling some lies
About his ideals. I tried to hide.

It was with relief that I realized the Rose Queen
Saw the irony too — that my lessons hadn't been
Totally lost. She thought it wrong it took
Drawings and stories to judge the boys, not looks
That her girlfriends at school were thought of as losers.

So, the lesson is, sisters, she'll respect what you taught her
Despite contradictions have faith in your daughter
You'll just about live through that day in the summer
When you too may be labelled "Rose Queen's mother".

No Bonking in the Corridors

We were the bouncers, see
at this disco
actually we were friends —
a fifteenth birthday party
a friend of a friend
to be frank
I was the mother

Disaster —
we did the right things
hired a hall
ghetto blasters
made food, watered the punch
threw out the drunks.

And the rules
well, they were clearly stated
"no puking, no fighting
no bonking in the corridors"

Well, I can say now
there was no fighting
the police came once
blaring and screeching
took away four boys
for stone throwing —
but, no fighting

Puking — well. I'm afraid there was
oceans of it
young men under threat
swished it round with mops

and smiled uneasily
retching became reassuring —
they hadn't died in our care

we became skilled with buckets
strategically placed
the light-on, records-off, police-are-coming, tactics
the hall emptied — except for the hopelessly drunk
the dog ate the biscuits and nuts

I prised a couple apart
lifting the tiny young man through the open door
while the heavily-breathing girl
cried "I love you, Gary"
puking over the floor

Much later
the girl fell off her chair
and hummed
and a lad full of punch
thought he was Rambo or Rocky V
we cleared up his illusions

Well, as mother-bouncer
I can say
I will laugh, given time
like several years, decades maybe

and I can say
thanks to the other bouncers
a colleague, a neighbour, a friend of a friend

there may well have been drunkenness
and limited debauchery
and certainly with drink and sick, the place was — well —
honking
but there was absolutely
absolutely
no bonking in the corridors.

i love you today

i love you today
perhaps not tomorrow or forever
i cannot say
today you seem the man for me
good-looking and adorable
a kiss, a laugh, desirable
i know i can be
totally and blissfully
in love today
but my ability
to promise you a deep romance
lasting love
or marriage in a year or two
is limited by doubt and chance
who knows
i may wake presently
to find your magic for me
disappeared at daybreak
just another man to take
and leave
with no regrets or sorrow
i will only promise
i love you for today
today you are the man for me
totally and blissfully
if this is not enough for you
you're thinking of a week, a month, a year or two
i'd say it's only fairy tales and dreams
that spin a yarn to make it seem
love really means
for years, for keeps, eternity
i can only offer
a sweet and brief security
i love you for today
today you are the man for me
totally and blissfully

Sixteen

Walking among the luke-warm puddles
with my high-heeled shoes in my hand
in the Saturday night-club crowds
I know I have met the man of my dreams

I know as I splash up the High Street
and the rain flattens my hair
I know as I climb the steep cobbled hill
with the swollen gutters
I know as my toes curl on the winter-warm pavement
and my glamorous shoes dangle on my lovely hand

This is my perfect evening of evenings
it must not end
He is all that I long for
and paddling along the terraces
I know he is sweetness love and life itself

I am sixteen and beautiful
and the moment is mine
I know I have met the man of my dreams
walking among the luke-warm puddles
with my high-heeled shoes in my hand

Advice on Pregnancy

What is pregnancy?
It's obviously an issue to be treated seriously
involving, as it does, the future of the human race.
The Magic of Pregnancy is much talked about
by men and superwomen
but here I offer a little practical advice
for the woman in the street.

First you will need the ability
to pee into a small bottle
accurately, before breakfast, and stop midstream
(remember to wash the bottle first or
expect a health visitor
relentlessly pursuing contaminated samples).

Secondly, an affinity with plastic dolls helps.
There are lots of these in the ante-natal clinic
all wearing nappies in different styles.

Thirdly acquire a thorough knowledge
of all the public loos —
exact location, cost and comfort.

Next, an ability to move bulk.
Placing a demi-john on a shelf
is good practise for travelling on a bus
Also try driving an overloaded lorry with care.

Fifth — Association.
Only associate with thin women
More than one pregnant/overweight woman
seen together
is a joke.

and sixth, don't let it show
or let it all show.
In pregnancy there is no middle way
a Bump is a Bump.

Seventh, don't worry about "Internals"
men are experienced at this kind of thing.

Lastly, *Learn the Signs*.
Chelsea buns and chips are *not* a normal meal
Five minute labour pains are not a) diarrheoa b) belated
    period pains c) cramp d) psychosomatic
Ignore advice that it's natural and doesn't hurt
also stories of African women and bushes —
these are the fantasies of male academics.
Note that the majority of husbands who faint during labour
    like large families
and that hospitals who want you to come again have a vested
    interest — ignore them.

and any advice to forget the pain, the inconvenience, the
    humiliation
WRITE IT DOWN

these are just some practical points to remember
about pregnancy and its magic.

Latch-key Kid

"But what will you do in the holidays" the interviewer said.
What indeed?
What was there to do with my sweet-natured, latch-key kid
but deny her existence
or rent or invent a granny or mother-in-law
or give up the idea of working at all?
"My first husband takes her to stay" I lied,
as though the country was crowded with cast-off husbands of
    mine
"we're on excellent terms".
I smooth down the fold of my pinafore dress
and blink at my brand new past.
The man rumbles on, like far away thunder,
"and after school, half term, what happens then?"

Ah, what happens then?

I flick through the years
playgroups and nurseries, childminders, neighbours and
    friends,
the impossible places reached on lumbering, always-late
    buses,
the hours that never quite matched with the hours at work,
the guilt,
the hum of exhaustion like telephone wires in the wind.

"My sister" I said, "she takes her",
"She lives down the road,
and my aunt on occasion, next door but one,
but anyway, Gran's in the attic,

I've an out-of-work nursery teacher renting the downstairs
    flat
and two substitute mothers on permanent call".

Well, what could he say?
That I lied?
That he didn't like communal living?
That I had too many family ties?
That he wanted somebody younger, more mobile?

Well, he did.

What *was* there to do with my sweet-natured, latch-key kid
but deny her existence?

a much-neglected art

we women who have so often felt alone
do not request acceptance
we do not ask anything at all

we read poems to our friends
keep diaries and letters hidden in the chest of drawers
play jazz piano in the back rooms of our homes
paint on the inside covers of our children's books

we sculpt exquisite curves on jugs and flower pots
and filling them with freshly-sharpened knives
we place them firmly
at the very centre of our lives

we do not *ask* anything at all

The Woman Who Knits

The woman who knits
is dangerous

he didn't realise that

he understood the obvious motion of needles
clacking into some kind of eternity
the intensity of fingers
dedicated to secret and intricate patterns
combined with the blank look at telly

he recognized the refusal to communicate
in anything but platitudes

he knew some of the signs

for instance, he knew the tendency
to start counting
when a difficult question arose
the changing of colours suddenly
at the punch line of his latest joke
muttering like some witches' chant
deep pink to scarlet red, dark blue to indigo

and half way up the sleeve
he knew a family row would bring a shout
"knit, pearl and tbl
yarn forward, two together
loop, decrease
and cast off three
on each alternate row"

that night he stayed out too late
and came in drunk
the stitches tightened
the tension changed
he thought she was
just knitting

and when
as was his usual way
he turned his back
he did not hear her yell
"join arm and neckband seams
cast off : don't press"

and next day
the jumper made
she'd gone

Perhaps I'm Normal Too

I didn't know another woman looked like me
I didn't know I wasn't a freak

I longed to be slim and neat
with stand-up breasts
and skin-tight jeans
on a small but cheeky bum
I longed for mini-skirt thighs
I longed to be petite or statuesque
I longed to be other than me

So when we swam together at Pwll Du
the sea entirely ours
I was surprised
to see you
broad and floppy, wide and sexy, plump and messy
just like me

I didn't know another woman looked that way
Perhaps your normal woman looks that way.
Perhaps I'm normal too.

I would be beautiful but . . .

I would be beautiful
but
my nose is much too long and straight
I would be beautiful
but
my hair's too fine
and going grey
I would be beautiful
but
my hips are rather big
to say the least
my shoulders much too small
my feet too broad
my breasts — they sag

I would be beautiful
but
it seems to me impossible
I'm no Fonda or Loren
and the work involved is tedious
the make-up exercise and perms
no mud no rain no sea
a careful sun
no drink no chips no honey-bun
but just
a sweet and perfect, strange and static me

I would be beautiful
but
beauty is skin-deep they say
and rather than await discovery
beneath all this abnormality
I'm opting for a destiny
with all my idiosyncracy
so I can say defiantly
"well — THIS IS ME"

On Becoming Forty : A Crisis of Confidence

it has taken years of careful neglect
to get this far

you don't think the garden looks like this by chance?
long grass and buttercups
cultivated carelessly
through whole summers
of forgetfulness
"like a meadow" I say with confidence

you don't think the house got this way
by chance?
all those carelessly draped shawls
the jungle of plants
the carefully hung cobwebs
the picturesque leak in the roof
no
it has taken years of careful neglect
to achieve all this
"the country look" I say with confidence

you don't think my daughter grew this way
by luck?
all those carefully planned non-sexist toddler groups
those creative flexible rules
laid down by a harrassed mum
all those survival skills she learned
as a latch key kid
all that insight into teenage culture
no
it has taken years of careful neglect
for her to grow this way
"go eat your heart out Dr Spock", I cry with confidence

don't think I am this way
by luck or chance
it has taken years of unplanned misadventure
to get this far
a passionate improvident romance
a love child
years of unexpected single parenthood
a whole career in hustling, hobbling, penny-pinching
a thousand daily dramas met head on
a hundred cracks and bumps
a dozen crises in which I crashed and thrashed about
until accidentally
I tumbled into middle age
celebrating forty wayward years —
with confidence

Mary's Dream

I

My dream is for all of us

I would like each one of us to be the heroine we only see in
    fantasy

The magazines and television would have us believe that we
    are heroines
                          "unsung heroines"
battling against impossible odds on the Great Domestic
    Front
slaying the ogres of Dust and Disorder with miracle products
    and patience

That way we stay in our homes and feel guilty about our
    dreams.

II

Yes —
we are the heroines for putting up with the low wages and the
                          endless housework
playing
    Mother
        Wife
            Madonna
                Worker
                    and Seductress
But our dreams belong not to Glyn's mother to Tracey's
                    mummy or to Mrs John Evan Jones
but to Meg and Joan and Isabel

47

III

I dream that we have a choice -
    to travel
        to have children
            to have no children
               to marry
                   to live alone
      to love women
        to love men
           to go into politics
              to sing and write
    to walk alone at night without fear
    to change the world
    to show compassion and kindness without it being
        assumed we should do it all for free

I dream that our choices are made from an infinite variety

not just being a Florence Nightingale
           a Mother Theresa
              or a Brigitte Bardot

not just Career Woman
         or Mother
            Superwoman
              or Housewife

IV

My dream is that I become famous so that I can say these
              things to a million people

I despise the drudgery and anonymity of being just another
    one-parent family in just another terraced house the same
    as its neighbour

I would love and despise the high life and glitter
as I love the quiet courage of the unsung heroines
but despise their passive tolerance and their acceptance that
                    their dreams will never become reality.

V

I dream like us all

but also I think of now

the changes we can make in our lives

the heroines of today.

Celebration Two:
Reaching for the Sky

with broad shoulders
we carry food and coal
with strong legs
we keep moving on
with powerful arms
we reach to the sky
with tough hands
we mould our lives

and through wide hips
our daughters are born.

HONNO
THE NEW WELSH WOMEN'S PRESS

HONNO has been set up by a group of women who feel that women in Wales have limited access to literature which relates specifically to them. The aim is to publish all kinds of books by women, in both English and Welsh including:

* fiction, poetry, plays, children's books
* research on Welsh women's history and culture
* reprints of out-of-print titles
* equal numbers of Welsh and English books.

HONNO is registered as a community co-operative. Any profit will go towards future publications. Shareholders' liability is limited to the amount invested. So far we have raised nearly £4000 by selling shares at £5 each to approximately 300 women from all over Wales and beyond. We hope that many more women will be able to help us in this way. Buy as many as you can – we need your support.

Each shareholder regardless of number of shares held, will have her say in the company and one vote at its AGM.

Although shareholding is restricted to women, we welcome gifts and loans of money from anyone.

If you would like to buy some shares or if you would like more information, write to:

HONNO, 'Ailsa Craig', Heol y Cawl, Dinas Powys, De Morgannwg, CF6 4AH